T0381321

To order additional copies of this book, contact:
Xlibris
844-714-8691
www.Xlibris.com
Orders@Xlibris.com

ISBN:	Softcover		978-1-5035-3183-3
		EBook			978-1-5035-3182-6

Print information available on the last page

Rev. date: 09/11/2020

Burrow Buddies

A Story About a True Symbiotic Friendship

Dr. Vicki Breazeale

Illustrated by Narae Kang

This photo is the real deal: the real characters in *Burrow Buddies*. Notice the tarantula (Dugesiella hentzi) with its front legs in the air protecting the toad (Gastrophryne olivacea) from the western ribbon snake (Thamnophis proximus). You too can discover very special relationships in nature; all you need to do is carefully and consistently observe the nature around you over time. Go for it! (Permission of Natural History Magazine)

Published aspects of the actual symbiosis and other established biological terms and processes are highlighted in blue.

Chapter One: Annie Names Poka

Annie Spits Poka Out of Her Mouth.

There once was a baby tarantula named Poka. Her mother didn't give her this name; Annie, her mother's burrow-buddy, named her. You see, when Poka was only one day old and very, very small, she got caught in Annie's mouth.

Luckily, Poka had bristles on her rear-end that poked Annie's tongue and made her spit Poka right out of her mouth! At the time, Annie was cleaning the burrow of invading bugs. She tried hard to avoid baby tarantulas while scooping bugs into her mouth, but Poka liked to be near Annie from the moment she hatched.

Annie and Poka Cleaning the Burrow of Pill Bigs.

Annie kept the burrow spic-and-span, but she wasn't your usual housekeeper. Annie was a toad! She was full grown, but Annie was a tiny toad.

True Happiness is a Clean, Comfortable Burrow.

Poka was only a month old, but she was already half Annie's size. Poka loved to spend her days with Annie in the warm, cozy burrow they called home. She was happy that Annie was her mother's best friend.

From the very beginning, there was a special bond between Poka (the baby tarantula) and Annie (the toad). Poka asked Annie more questions than all of her hundreds of brothers and sisters combined (spiders have many babies all at once). "Annie, why do you live with a family of tarantulas instead of toads? Where are your parents? Do you have any babies? Why do you keep our burrow clean?"

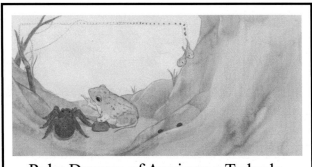
Poka Dreams of Annie as a Tadpole.

Annie always tried to answer as many of Poka's questions as possible. Annie didn't really know who her parents were, but she thought she saw them one day when she was a tiny tadpole. "What's a tadpole?" asked Poka.

"It's what I was before I became a toad," Annie replied. This fascinated Poka. She wanted to meet a baby tadpole someday. She wanted to see a tadpole become a toad!

Poka Learns about Spider School.

When Poka was two months old and Annie's size, Poka's mother told her that in two weeks she would begin spider school. At first, Poka didn't want to go to school because she would be away from Annie, who had already taught her almost everything she needed to know.

Besides, Annie always shared her pill bugs with Poka. Both toads and tarantulas love pill bugs!

Chapter Two: Poka Begins Spider School

Soon enough, the first day of school arrived. Poka was excited and couldn't stop asking her mother questions about school. One thing Poka was full of was questions. "What am I going to learn that Annie hasn't already taught me? Who will be my teacher? Will I meet other spiders? Will anyone with fewer than eight legs be there?"

Proud Poka at Spider School.

Poka arrived at school and saw more kinds of spiders at school than she could count. There were wolf spiders, trap-door spiders, jumping spiders, and many more, but she and her brothers and sisters were the largest spiders of all. This made Poka proud and gave her a new sense of responsibility.

There were twenty different spiderlings in Poka's class. She was seated on a leaf next to a cute little trap-door spider named Sally. Sally looked a lot like Poka. She had eight eyes (1 big one and 3 small ones on either side of her head), but she didn't have any bristles on her

Poka Meets Sally and Dr. Bug.

rear-end. They talked until a pink-toed spider with green glasses walked to the center of the class and announced, "I'm your teacher -- Dr. Bug, but you can call me Vicki."

Dr. Bug told them, "You will learn how to balloon, dig burrows, build webs, and even create internet web pages in spider school.

You need to pay attention and master all of the spider skills for your species because you cannot graduate from school until you pass the S.A.T., the Spider Attitude Test. Are there any questions?"

"What's a species?" asked Poka.

Dr. Bug Talks about Spider School.

Dr. Bug replied, "What is your name, little spiderling? Please help all of us learn your name by saying it before you ask a question."

Poka responded, "My name is Poka Dot and my question is, What is a species?" except members of your same *species*."

Dr. Bug replied, "Excellent question, Poka Dot. A species is a unique living thing that is not exactly like any other. You are a member of a group of spiders called *tarantulas*, but you are a unique kind

The Spiderlings Learn About Species.

of tarantula like no other. No other tarantulas look and act exactly like you except members of your same species."

"Like my mom and my brothers and sisters!" announced Poka.

"Exactly right," said Dr. Bug.

Spiderlings Line Up for Ballooning Practice.

"Today, those of you who want to balloon will practice ballooning. The rest of you will help the ballooners. Please form a line behind me from tallest to shortest spider." Poka and Sally were the first spiderlings in line behind Dr. Bug.

"Now, I want willing ballooners to raise your first right foot. Keep your feet in the air until a nonballooner buddies up with you," said Dr. Bug. Amazingly, there were exactly 10 ballooners and 10 nonballooners! When there were no more feet in the air, Dr. Bug continued, "Follow me up to the top of the Coyote bush. Once you're at the top, spread out so that each pair of you is on a different leaf."

Ballooners and Non-Ballooners Pair Up.

Once everyone was on a leaf, Dr. Bug said, "Ballooners, make sure your spinnerets are working by casting a few threads of silk into the air. Whistle if you need help. When everyone is ready, I will count to three and non- ballooners will gently push ballooners off the leaves!"

Spiderlings Try Their Spinnerets.

When everyone was ready, Dr. Bug announced, "Ready? One, two, three..., **Push**!" All at once, the ballooners sailed through the air, gently floating to the ground on a thin thread of of silk. Wow, what a beautiful sight! Not a single spiderling landed belly up. They practiced ballooning until it was time to go home.

Spiderlings Balloon for the First Time.

Chapter Three: Poka and Sally Become Best friends

Poka and Sally walked home from school together and discovered that their burrows were on opposite sides of the oldest Saguaro cactus in the desert. Living in the shadow of *Gramps*, as they fondly called the old Saguaro, was a very special place. They played on their way home and became best friends.

Poka and Sally Become Friends.

Sally Spots Annie in Poka's Burrow.

As they got close to Poka's burrow, they saw Annie peeking out of the door. Poka jumped for joy to see Annie and ran to greet her. Poka had much to tell Annie about her first day at spider school.

"Poka, what's that green thing peeking out of your burrow?" asked Sally.

Poka quickly replied, "Guess you can't see well, even though you have eight eyes! That's not a thing! That's Annie, my mom's best friend and my best buddy. She lives with us and she's a toad."

"That's the silliest thing I have ever heard in my life," said Sally. "Spiders don't live with toads. They eat 'em! You can't be friends with something you eat," said Sally. "Wait until I tell Dr. Bug about this! You'll find out that you can *not* be friends with anything green!"

Poka paid no attention to Sally. She was already gently touching Annie's back with one of her eight feet. This was the best way to make sure it was indeed Annie and not an impostor toad. You see, tarantulas have tiny hairs that can smell like noses on the bottoms of their feet and, even though they have eight eyes, they can't see very well.

Poka Fondly Greets Annie.

The next day, Sally got to school before Poka and loudly told Dr. Bug that Poka was in love with a toad! The other spiderlings heard Sally's announcement. By the time Poka got to school, everyone was talking about her.

She was teased about her love for a *four-legged green thing* the whole day. Poka walked home from school alone, wouldn't speak to anyone in the burrow, even Annie, and went to sleep without eating one pill bug!

Sally Gossips about Poka's Love for Annie.

The next morning Poka felt even worse than the day before. Tears were dripping from her eyes as she told her mother about what had happened at school the day before.

Poka's mom gently touched Poka's back with one of her feet. "Dry your eyes, little spiderling. There is no reason to cry. Our species of tarantula love toads like Annie because it's natural and a good thing to do! Ask Dr. Bug to explain the details of our relationship with toads to you and your classmates in spider school today." This made Poka happy again. Her mother was wise and wonderful.

Poka Cries.

Chapter Four: Poka Sees Green

Poka walked to school slowly and observed everything in her path carefully, with a new sense of wonder. She noticed for the first time that the world was very green. She noticed that all the

Poka Sees Green for the First Time!

plants were green and asked out loud, "Why are plants green? What would the world be like without green things?" She realized that if she was green she could sit quietly on a leaf and no one would see her. She could do many wonderful things if she was green. "I wish I was green!" she shouted to the world as she

made her way to school.

Poka was late to school. All of her classmates were busy talking when she arrived because Dr. Bug was also late. They were gossiping about Poka and Annie. As she sat down next to Sally, one of the

Dr. Bug Turns Green!

spiderlings shouted, "Are you still in love with that green toad named Annie?"

Before Poka could respond, a green spider with pink toes and green glasses entered the classroom. Everyone stopped talking and stared at the green spider. "Who are you?" one

of the spiderlings asked.

The green spider replied, "You don't recognize me! I'm Dr. Bug. How do you like me green?"

The class sat silent and stunned. Finally, Poka spoke. "On my way to school, I was thinking that I could do many wonderful things if I were green." Dr. Bug smiled at Poka and asked, "If you're not green yourself, what's the next best thing?"

Poka knew the answer and replied, "Having a green buddy like Annie!"

"Poka, you are a smart little spiderling. It is indeed wonderful to have a green buddy like Annie. However, the relationship that your species of tarantula (*Dugesiella hentzi*) has with Annie's species of toad (*Gastrophryne olivacea*) is a friendship that has been growing for a very long time. It probably began with your great-great-great-great-great-great-great grandma (7 great grandmas) and Annie's great-great-great-great-great-great grandma (6 great grandmas)!"

Dr. Bug continued, "It's called a symbiotic relationship *or* the living together of two very different species. And, your symbiosis is the best kind of all because it is good for both species. How does Annie help your Mom and your family, Poka?" asked Dr. Bug.

Dr. Bug Explains Symbiosis.

"Well, Annie eats every bug that comes into our burrow and lots of bugs come in, especially when it's hot and dry outside. It would be hard to sleep if Annie didn't stop the bugs from taking over the burrow," responded Poka. "And what does your Mom do for Annie in return?" asked Dr. Bug.

Poka could not answer this question and said, "I don't really know what my Mom does for Annie. Do you know, Dr. Bug?"

"I do indeed," responded Dr. Bug. "Your mother protects Annie from the western ribbon snake (*Thamnophis proximus*) who would like to make a meal out of Annie."

"I didn't know that," said Poka. "I've never seen a ribbon snake."

Chapter Five: Annie Is Missing

Poka ran home from school as fast as her eight legs would carry her. She couldn't wait to tell her mother and Annie about the very special symbiotic relationship they had.

Annie is Missing!

As Poka neared the burrow, she could see her mother pacing back and forth in front of the burrow door. As she got even closer, she could here her mother crying, "Annie, Annie, where are you? Come home, Annie! We need you, Annie! Please come home!!!"

This made Poka run even faster, and she yelled to her mother as she ran, "Mom, Mom, is Annie lost?"

Poka's mother was holding back her tears as she explained to Poka that Annie had been missing all day. "Annie followed you to school because she was worried about you. Now, I'm worried about Annie!"

Poka's brothers and sisters gathered around Poka's mother as they arrived home from school. "Let's all search for Annie. When you spot her, whistle as loud as you can until the rest of us find you. Be careful and be back in the burrow before dark, even if you don't find Annie!" said Poka's mom in a trembling voice.

Poka took off like a lightening bolt, looking for Annie and calling, "Annie, Annie! Where are you, Annie?" as she ran. A half hour later, Poka realized that she was lost, too! She had paid no attention to the path she was taking in her quest for Annie. As Poka thought about the pickle she was in, she heard a whistle in the distance. "Annie has been found!" she shouted. "I'll just head toward the whistle until I'm found, too!"

Poka is Lost.

As Poka made her way to the whistle, she spotted a large group of tarantulas in the distance. Her mother and another tarantula were arguing and all of their children were gathered around the angry pair.

"What's going on?" Poka asked one of her brothers. "Mom found Annie eating barbecued pill bug kabobs right here at our neighbor's burrow! Mom wants Annie to come home, but our neighbor wants Annie to stay," her brother said.

Annie is Found.

Finally, Annie spoke up. "I am Mrs. Dot's best friend and burrow buddy. I want to go home with her to *our* burrow," Annie announced.

Poka's mom was happy that Annie had ended the argument. "Let's go home, spiderlings," she said.

Poka, all of her bothers and sisters, and Annie followed Poka's mom home. They were chattering with joy as they passed Gramps and filed into the burrow. "Go to bed. Tomorrow is the last day of school. All of you will be graduating," said Poka's mom.

Chapter Six: Poka is the Arachnatorian

The next morning, all of the spiderlings were up early brushing their bristles. Everyone was excited about graduation day. They had all passed the SAT (Spider Attitude Test) and were ready to begin life on their own.

Spiderlings Get Ready for Graduation.

Poka met Sally on the way to school. "Who do you think will be arachnatorian of the class?" Sally asked Poka.

"Beats me" said Poka. "I'm just happy that my mom and Annie will be there."

Sally responded, "Wow, I didn't know that Annie was coming to graduation. That's special!" This made Poka feel so happy that she felt like painting herself green; Sally wanted to be Annie's buddy, too! Dr. Bug was waiting for them when they arrived at school. She greeted every spiderling with a big smile and told them to sit down for graduation instructions. Poka and Sally could barely contain themselves, they were so happy and sad at the same time.

Graduation Day.

When all the spiderlings were seated, Dr. Bug began, "After all of your families are seated, I will give a short welcome and then hand out your de- grees, one spiderling at a time. Are there any questions?"

Sally raised her foot. "Yes, Sally, what's your question?" asked Dr. Bug.

"Who is the arachnatorian of the class?" asked Sally.

Dr. Bug responded with a question, "Which of your classmates do you think deserves highest honors for attitude? Which of you has displayed the most love for others? Which of you has maintained a good attitude no matter what?"

> *Note:* All spiders, tarantulas included, live very solitary lives; They come together once a year to make babies and spend the rest of the time alone.

Sally knew the answer to that question and replied, "Ms. Poka Dot has displayed a positive attitude, even though everyone gave her a bad time for loving a green toad named Annie."

Poka is the Arachnatorian!

Dr. Bug responded, "Sally, I agree with you whole- heartedly. How many of the rest of you agree with Sally?" All of the spiderl- ings raised both of their front feet and clapped for Poka, their arachnatorian!

Poka was caught by surprise.She hadn't given a thought to who would be the arachnatorian. She was flabbergasted! "Do I have to give a speech?" asked Poka.

Dr. Bug responded, "It would be wonderful if you would give a speech, Poka. We will all help you write and rehearse it. There will be no need for shaky knees or dry book lungs!"

> *Note:* All big spiders have "book lungs" that open up like the pages of a book in their knee joints to help them breathe.

The rest of the day passed quickly for Poka. Before she knew it, she was leading her fellow spiderlings before their families and friends, who were ready for the graduation to begin. Dr. Bug welcomed everyone and handed out degrees to each spiderling one-by- one before announcing, "Ms. Poka Dot, the arachnatorian, will now speak." Poka was nervous as she faced the crowd of adult spiders.

"My fellow spiderlings helped me prepare a speech, but instead of talking, I would like to introduce my best buddy, Annie. If it weren't for Annie, I wouldn't be the arachnatorian. Annie has taught me to love and respect other living things. I am happy to know Annie and I want you to know her, too!" proclaimed Poka.

The Spiderling Graduate from Spider School.

Annie joined Poka and the other graduates. "It is an honor to be here with so many spiders who don't want to eat me!" Annie said with a laugh and continued. "You must be proud of your spiderlings. They have indeed learned a lot in spider school.

Annie Gets Hugged.

They are ready to take their place in the world." One by one, each spiderling gave Annie a hug.

Chapter Seven: Poka Saves Annie

Poka tried to keep up with Annie as her family slowly made their way home after graduation from spider school. Annie could hop a good distance with her strong back legs and was always several paces ahead of the rest. She disappeared over a big mound before Poka could catch up with her. On the other side of the mound, Annie came face to face with a western ribbon snake. The snake was hungry and very happy to see Annie.

As Poka arrived at the top of the mound, she saw the encounter and ran to help Annie. She quickly got between Annie and the snake. Immediately, Poka reared up on her back legs with her front legs in the air and her fangs ready to pounce. Upon seeing the mighty Poka, the snake slid away in a hurry. Poka's mother and brothers and sisters saw the scene from the top of the mound and cheered as the snake departed.

Poka Saves Annie.

Chapter Eight: Annie Has Tadpoles

Poka spent the summer close to Annie. They talked about many things, especially about Poka's future. There were many summer rain storms and Poka saw lightening and heard thunder for the first time.

Poka and Annie Spend the Summer Together.

During the summer, Annie was away for a whole week. Poka's mom said that Annie was making babies. Poka was very curious about Annie's babies. She remembered that she had asked Annie about her parents and ba- bies when she was a little spiderling. Annie had said that she was a tadpole before she became a toad. Poka could not understand how a tadpole could become a toad.

Poka Sees Tadpoles Metamorphose into Toads.

When Annie returned to the burrow, Poka begged to see her babies. Finally, Annie agreed to take Poka to the seasonal pond nearby where all of the toads went to have babies.

The pond was full of tadpoles! They looked like fish, but some of them had legs. As Poka looked more closely, she could see that tadpoles do indeed become toads because there were tadpoles in all stages of the process in the pond.

Poka was amazed at the sight. She remembered that Dr. Bug had told her class that toads and frogs go through a dramatic change called metamorphosis in which they *morph* from a fish form that lives in water to a toad with legs that lives on land.

Three little toads that still had tadpole tails came up to Poka and Annie. "Hello, Mom!" said all of the baby toads at the same time.

Annie was surprised and responded, "Hi, sweetie pies! It's great to see you."

Poka immediately added, "Hello, babies. I'm one of your mom's best buddies. Would you like to come home with us?"

Poka and Annie Meet Annie's Babies.

All of the baby toads said, "Yes, yes!"

The baby toads followed Poka and Annie back to the burrow. Everyone in the burrow was happy to see them. Having Annie's babies there made the burrow feel more like home than ever before.

Chapter Nine: Poka Leaves Home

It was October 15th and it was getting colder. The sun was setting earlier and earlier each day. Poka knew that she must leave her mother's burrow very soon. She also knew that she would never return. She would never see Annie again. A tear dropped from each of her eight eyes.

Hibernation Time.

Poka's brothers and sisters had already left home to begin life on their own. Poka was the last spiderling in the burrow. She was sad to leave because life with Annie and her mom was wonderful. She could not imagine a better place to be. But the burrow was crowded with two adult tarantulas and four toads! Squeak and Beak, two of Annie's baby toads, loved Poka and followed her everywhere.

Poka Decides to Build a Burrow of Her Own.

October 18th was a paticularly cold day. Poka's mom was sleepy and wanted to close the burrow door for the winter very soon. "Poka, my dear spiderling, you must dig a burrow and make a life of your own. It's time to hibernate for the winter. You don't need to go very

far. There is a beautiful Saguaro cactus almost as old as Gramps nearby. Why don't you take Squeak and Beak with you and build a burrow there?"

Poka Makes a Home with Squeak and Beak.

Poka realized that she would have a wonderful life with Squeak and Beak. "Let's go build a burrow!" Poka announced to the two eager toads. They kissed their moms good-bye and left the burrow, with Squeak and Beak one hop ahead of the now happy Poka.

The End

Biographies

Author **Vicki Breazeale**, Ph.D. (Dr. Bug), is a science educator, inventor and Academic Director of the Integrated Science Program, an innovative weekend, accelerated science curriculum for students interested in pursuing degrees in health professions or biological sciences. She has taught biology and ecology in diverse settings to people of all ages for nearly three decades, including lecturing in Biology 1 for majors at UC Berkeley for 7 years. She also directed an innovative science education program serv- ing pre-health professionals in San Francisco, Los Angeles and St Louis for New College of California for 18 years. Vicki has extensive experience in formal and free-choice science curriculum design, implementation and evaluation. For example, Vicki developed and implemented a middle and elementary school curriculum on the natural history and ecology of San Francisco Bay for the California Academy of Sciences in San Francisco's Golden Gate Park and led nature field trips at the Lawrence Hall of Science in Berkeley. Vicki was the first person to describe a key allosteric enzyme in the Calvin Cycle of plants: Sedoheptulose 1,7 Bisphosphatase. In 2006, Vicki and colleagues founded Great Wilderness, a nonprofit whose mission is to support people living in the rich biodiversity of tropical bioregions where the preservation of natural ecosystems is critical to sustaining life. Vicki has a comprehensive knowledge of biology, as well as a detailed understanding of cognitive development and learning theories. She has a B.S., M.S., and Ph.D. from the University of California, Berkeley.

www.integratedscienceprogram.com
www.greatwilderness.org
doctorbug@earthlink.net

Narae Kang is a free lance illustrator in Upstate New York.

Testimonial

Burrow Buddies was used in the First Grade Class of the Belle Sherman School in Ithaca, NY by Mrs. Ellen Falkson during the 2008/9 school year. She found that students of varying preparation could all benefit. Some just liked the illustrations and listening to it being read; some read it avidly to themselves or even to other students. The combination of good science, great illustrations, and a compelling story line all add to its impact. And, the societal impact of living and working with beings of all types was not lost on students and staff. Belle Sherman has a demographic in which Caucasian students only make up about 50% of the student body.